Wish Fish

Written by Sam Hay
Illustrated by Katie May

WISE WALRUS

What is synthetic phonics?

Synthetic phonics teaches children to recognise the sounds of letters and to blend 'synthesise' them together to make whole words.

Understanding sound/letter relationships gives children the confidence and ability to read unfamiliar words, without having to rely on memory or guesswork; this helps them progress towards independent reading.

Did you know? Spoken English uses more than 40 speech sounds. Each sound is called a *phoneme*. Some phonemes relate to a single letter (d-o-g) and others to combinations of letters (sh-ar-p). When a phoneme is written down it is called a *grapheme*. Teaching these sounds, matching them to their written form and sounding out words for reading is the basis of synthetic phonics.

Consultant

I love reading phonics has been created in consultation with language expert Dr Marlynne Grant (Chartered and Registered Educational Psychologist). For more than 25 years, Marlynne has worked as a regional educational psychologist, specialising in literacy development for children of all abilities.

Reading tips

Wish Fish focuses on the **sh** sound.

Tricky words in *Wish Fish*

Any words in bold do not sound exactly as they look (don't fit the usual sound-letter rAles) or are new and have not yet been introduced.

Tricky words in this book:

she   **s<u>ai</u>d**   **I**   **o<u>f</u>**   **m<u>y</u>**

w<u>a</u>s   **<u>the</u>**   **p<u>u</u>sh**   **w<u>e</u>**

Extra ways to have fun with *Wish Fish!*

After the reader has read the story, ask them questions about what they have just read:

What does Meg find in the pond?
Why does Meg wish that she doesn't have a wish fish?

Explain that the two letters 'sh' make one sound. Think of other words that use the 'sh' sound, such as ship or shop.

I love reading.
I have lots of books
but I always wish
for more!

A pronunciation guide

This grid contains the sounds used in the story and a guide on how to say them.

s as in sat	**a** as in ant	**t** as in tin	**p** as in pig
i as in ink	**n** as in net	**c** as in cat	**e** as in egg
h as in hen	**r** as in rat	**m** as in mug	**d** as in dog
g as in get	**o** as in ox	**u** as in up	**l** as in log
f as in fan	**b** as in bag	**v** as in van	**w** as in wet
y as in yet	**qu** as in quiz	**x** as in box	**ff** as in off
ll as in fill	**ck** as in duck	**sh** as in shop	

Be careful not to add an 'uh' sound to 's', 't', 'p', 'c', 'h', 'r', 'm', 'd', 'g', 'l', 'f' and 'b'. For example, say 'fff' not 'fuh' and 'sss' not 'suh'.

Meg is at a pond. **She** has a net.

Pip has got a ship.

'A fish!' **said** Meg.
'**I** am a wish fish,' it **said**.

'Gosh!' **said** Meg.

'**I** wish **I** had a lot **of** cash,'
said Meg.

Pop! Meg got a shock.
'A sack **of** cash!' **she said**.

'**I** wish **my** ship **was** big,'
said Pip.

Pop! **The** ship is big.
But it has a bad fox on it.

'**I** spot cash,' **said** Fox.
Fox got off **the** ship.

'Stop him!' **said** Meg.
'Fox will rob us!'

Pip is quick. **Push**!

Fox is wet. Fox is mad!

'Quick!' **said** Pip. 'A wish!'

'**I** wish **I** had not got a wish fish,'
said Meg.

Pop! **The** wish fish, cash and Fox
vanish. **The** ship is not big.

Meg is sad. '**We** can get a pet fish and a big ship at a shop,' **said** Pip.

'Yes. But not a fox!' **said** Meg.

Other **Level 2** titles to enjoy:

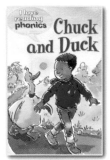

978-1-84898-387-8

978-1-84898-389-2

978-1-84898-388-5

Other titles in the series

Level **1**

978-1-84898-277-2   978-1-84898-396-0   978-1-84898-390-8   978-1-84898-391-5

Level **3**

978-1-84898-397-7

978-1-84898-398-4

978-1-84898-399-1

978-1-84898-400-4

Copyright © Wise Walrus Ltd 2011
First published in Great Britain in 2011 by Wise Walrus
The Pantiles Chambers, 85 High Street, Tunbridge Wells, Kent TN1 1XP
ISBN: 978-1-84898-386-1
Printed in China 10 9 8 7 6 5 4 3 2 1